dancing lessons
for the
advanced in age

Also by Bohumil Hrabal

THE LITTLE TOWN WHERE TIME STOOD STILL

TOO LOUD A SOLITUDE

THE DEATH OF MR. BALTISBERGER

CLOSELY WATCHED TRAINS

I SERVED THE KING OF ENGLAND

dancing lessons
for the
advanced in age

bohumil hrabal

TRANSLATED FROM THE CZECH BY

MICHAEL HENRY HEIM

HARCOURT BRACE & COMPANY

New York   San Diego   London

This is a translation of Taneční hodiny pro starší a pokročilé

Library of Congress Cataloging-in-Publication Data
Hrabal, Bohumil, 1914–
[Taneční hodiny pro starší a pokročilé. English]
Dancing lessons for the advanced in age: a novel/Bohumil Hrabal;
translated from the Czech by Michael Henry Heim.—1st ed.
p.   cm.
ISBN 0-15-123810-3
I. Heim, Michael Henry.   II. Title.
PG5039.18.R2T313   1995
891.8'635—dc20   95-11762

Designed by Trina Stahl
Printed in the United States of America
First edition
A B C D E

Not only may one imagine that what is higher derives always and only from what is lower; one may imagine that—given the polarity and, more important, the ludicrousness of the world—everything derives from its opposite: day from night, frailty from strength, deformity from beauty, fortune from misfortune. Victory is made up exclusively of beatings.

— LADISLAV KLÍMA

dancing lessons
for the
advanced in age

JUST LIKE I COME HERE TO SEE YOU, young ladies, I used to go to church to see my beauties, well, not exactly to church, I'm not much of a churchgoer, but to a small shop next to the parish house, a tiny little place, where a man by the name of Altman sold secondhand sewing machines, dual-spring Victrolas from America, and Minimax fire extinguishers, and this Altman he had a sideline delivering beauties to pubs and bars all over the district, and the young ladies would sleep in Altman's back room, or when summer came they set up tents in the garden and the dean of the church would take his constitutional along the fence and those show-offs would put a Victrola out there and sing and smoke and tan themselves in their bathing suits, a sight for sore eyes it was, a heavenly sight, Eden on earth, which is why the dean took all those inspection tours along the fence, that and the rotten luck he had with his priests, one ran off to Canada with his cousin, another converted to the Czechoslovak Church, and a third defied his ban and climbed the fence, fell in love with one of the beauties, and shot himself out of unrequited love, revolver or Browning, it always gets you in the end, we borrowed one when we were boys and shot at the fence like Conar Tolnes, but then my brother took it apart and we couldn't put it back together, we were so desperate we wanted to shoot ourselves, but we couldn't because we couldn't put it back together, a good thing too or I wouldn't have been able to go to church to see the ladies, I was always dressed to kill, striped trousers like a bank clerk, and sat on a Minimax case like a diplomat, the sun beating down, the ladies lolling in bathing suits on blankets like a sun worshipers' society, six of them flat on their backs, cradling their heads—wigs and all—in their hands, gazing up into the clouds, delivering their bodies to men's eyes, and because I was as sensitive as Mozart and an admirer of the European Renaissance I stared at them like a crocodile, one eye on the dean, the other on their crossed legs and dangling ankles, the shivers that ran down my spine, how many people get to see so many beauties in one place? only emperors or sultans, anyway, I'd tell the ladies my dreams, like the one where the baker puts his loaf into the oven, which means winning the lottery, a pity I had no ticket, dreaming of a bakery means nocturnal revels, though what good is that? neither Havlíček nor Christ ever laughed, if anything they wept, because when you stand for a great idea you can't horse around, Havlíček had a brain like a diamond, the professors went gaga over him, they tried to make him a bishop, but no, he chose justice, a little coffee, a little wine, and a life for the people, stamping out illiteracy, only

perverse people dream of rolling in manure (better days ahead) or of chamber pots (your future
is assured) because the thing is, dear ladies, you've
got to rely on yourselves, take Manouch, who
thought he had it made because his father was a
jailer and all he did was drink and pick up bad
habits, which leads to fights like the quarrel in
the days of the monarchy between the social democrats and the freethinkers and clerics over
whether the world comes from a monkey or God
slapped Adam together out of mud and fashioned
Eve from his insides, now He could have made
her out of mud too, it would have been cheaper,
though nobody really knows what went on, the
world was as deserted as a star, but people twitter
away like magpies and don't really care, I could
set my sights on a charmer, a prime minister's
daughter, but what's not to be is not to be and
could even take a bad turn, Mother of God! the
crown prince had syphilis and that Vetsera
woman shot him, but then *she* got shot by the

coachman, though any young lady will tell you you might as well be buried alive if the man in your life has a faulty fandangle, when I was serving in the most elegant army in the world I told our medical officer, Doctor, I said, I've got a weak heart, but all he said was, So have I, boy, and if we had a hundred thousand like you we could conquer the world, and he put me into the highest category, so I was a hero, I walked out of there on cloud nine, but he called me back and said, You've got time on your hands, take my wife to the station, she was a beauty, his wife, the spitting image of Mařenka Zieglerová and a giant like Maria Theresa and dressed like a queen too, and the first words out of her mouth were, Are you a bachelor? and when it was over she tried to give me a tip, six kreuzers, but I wouldn't take it, that's called chivalry, Havlíček and Christ wouldn't have taken one either, we had a real thing about appearances back then, I wore a pince-nez and a tie-clip made from a medal a friend of my grandfather's got for winning the high jump at the Achilles Sport Club in Brno, but the main thing was money, you could get anything for money, beautiful women, you might be a hunchback or getting on in years, but you could buy a real beauty, it's just how the world turns round the universe, and even though I've pledged allegiance to emperors and presidents I'm still a hero, I've still got my magic hands, my surgeon's hands, a shoemaker always has fine hands, and people call me a real professional, Baťa himself wrote me a letter begging me to work for him and put his business back on its feet, and the Baroness Břízová, who used to get her milk from us, would look at me, lower her eyes, and say, You're one of us, aren't you? and she was as noble as they come, with a tiny little face like the kittens on the chocolate bars, her daughter married that handsome Judge Just, the one known for throwing the book at all the rowdies and drunks, Tónek Opletalů once boxed his ears because he gave him thirteen months for slitting Říha's throat during an academic debate, but Christ, healer of nations and mainstay of the poor, knew way back then that man, predisposed as he is to villainy, soon sheds tears, which is why he had the strength to load that girder on his back for us all and lug it the two kilometers to Golgotha, all bloody and bruised, to this day priests go wild at the thought of it, though they prefer telling children about the Holy Trinity and how the Father is His own Son and the Son His Father and They use a messenger pigeon to communicate, it's enough to make your head spin, as if they didn't have their share of that stuff in the confessional, stepfathers and sons born out of wedlock, I mean, people don't like hearing it, because Christ wanted us to love our neighbors, he wanted discipline, not love on the sofa the way some mealy-brained idiots would have it, but I can be proud, I always kept the image of Havlíček before me and as a shoemaker I was always an engineer of human feet, the stitching was always white waxed thread, the nails never scratched the skin, I used only Elbet glue and gum dragon mixed with ground elephant hooves, but public opinion is made by idiots and drunks, I'd like to see them do a handstand on a horse at the age of seventy like our dearly departed President Masaryk, to say nothing of the Tibetan monks who are building a power station to illuminate the living Buddha, the tiny child Buddha, in their monastery, or Professor Einstein, who invented the atomic submarine, or the Russians, who are jetting around the world so fast that they have to put on their brakes the moment they take off and one speed engineer says the time is near when a jet will see its own tail flying around the earth and passengers won't even have a chance to sit down before arrival, they might as well stay home, but the main thing is not to live in a pigsty and to keep the ladies supplied with flowers, when our priest had trouble doing number one Doctor Karafiát said, If I've told you once I've told you a thousand times, bland foods only, no meat, no wine, and when a woman who'd just had a baby ate a sausage, he blew his top, Apples not good enough for you? he yelled and gave her husband an enema, because he should have known better than to let a woman in childbed even go near a sausage, when I went to Doctor Karafiát for my tapeworm, he put me on a diet and prescribed milk baths, other doctors would have shown me the door, but Doctor Karafiát said, The minute I saw you I could tell you were supersensitive and not cut out for holy matrimony, and it just happened to be market day and a woman was biting into a liverwurst when all of a sudden the doctor's dog ran out and tore the liverwurst and her lip away from her and Doctor Karafiát had to buy her another liverwurst and sew her lip back on because she ran bawling to him and men were still gallant in those days, a professor once said to me, We never gave the monarchy its due, he said, We never gave the

brothels their due, our men had too much vital
force in them, it made them supersensitive, Gru-
léšek would beat his wife with cats or catkins,
which is what loggers used to call the chains they
tied logs to their carts with, the lawyer who han-
dled the sale of our house, Kir his name was, built
a mansion for himself next to the courthouse
complete with fountains and palm trees and a
marble column topped by a naked Eve with the
whole world at her feet and her own rose garden,
anyway this lawyer shot himself because his wife
threw him over for a poor student, it was like an
operetta, rich ladies are always romantic, the of-
fers I used to get would make me break out something awful, of course I'll make you another pair
of shoes, I'll put on my magnifying glasses, KB-
model pumps, white lining, white insoles, number
four cut, Derby-Pariser line, one pair of pumps
with white toe caps and patent-leather heels, two
centimeters high, nickel-plate eyelets, celluloid
hooks, brass nails and brass screws to hold the

soles in place, and then I'll make you a spare pair of autumn shoes and a spare pair of winter shoes and line them with red or yellow lamb's wool, as you prefer, and a pair of walking shoes for hills and a pair of walking shoes for dales with matching red toe caps and white linings or in kidskin with trimming yea high and a green varnish, and I'll go all the way to Vienna, to Salamander, the mecca of the shoe world, five full floors of shoes, I'll go all that way for their Maitzen varnishes, varnishes as smooth as a beautiful face, Salamander, the mecca of the shoe world, with a salamander in its trademark, like the monkey in the Mercedes trademark, glass cases of shoes made by magic hands, each floor lit in a different color, Count Zelikowski would sail over the parade ground on his stallion like a fighter plane, his beard fringed with hoarfrost, his horse's mane too, he was known for his cruelty, was the count, once an old woman stopped and asked me what company her son was in, she'd made some cakes for him, and suddenly up rode Count Zelikowski on his stallion and roared, Who told you you could talk to that hag, you whoreson? and gave me a taste of his crop and leaped clear over the woman on his stallion at twenty degrees below zero, and once I was on guard duty, I was twenty-one at the time and so full of energy I could have lit Prague for a week, why, even now I'm a holy terror when I see that safeguard of marital bliss, a well-developed female body, and back then I was a member of the Sokol Gymnastic Society and had Sokol curls and a Sokol uniform that fit me like the president's fit him, and there was a whole field full of Sokols and flags waving in the trees, a row of white horses, a row of red horses, and two beauties tearing each other's blouses to shreds over me, but I had read my Batista, so I knew that if you hold nothing sacred you are open to sin and there are women who fall for love and women who fall for money and women who fall for both, there are women who

indulge in debauchery and women who indulge
in fads and women who indulge in artists, but
marriage is meant to be what Master Jan Hus said
it was, don't show leg, girls, until you know who
the boy really is, though the best thing is to keep
your word, which is why the Hindus have bulls
in their temples and bow down to them, the sibyl
who prophesied Christ's death was afraid to walk
the footbridge over the Jordan and bowed down
to the cedar it came from, and when her friends
asked her, Why won't you go? she said that one
day the bridge would be made into a cross and
she would rather wade across the river, skirt in
hand, she could see the cross embedded in the
bridge and she knew that Christ would come and
teach people that they are one another's brothers,
yes, she was a wise one, as wise as our own Saint
Wenceslas who so loved his vineyards and rode a
white horse in a white robe and gave to the poor
like a welfare state, now the Chinese they believe
in a god of strength and love, which is why their

god wears a gold ring in his nose, has a mouth like a shark, and is so big and fat he scares the bejesus out of you, whereas the Africans are more poetic, they believe in what they can eat and they leap and shout while their king sits naked on the throne with a pitchfork in his hand and their queen wears only a strip of cloth to keep the flies off her biomass, and when one of them dies they bury half the body and dig into the other, so Holub the travel photographer hopped on his bicycle lickety-split, and the Butacutos and the Arabelis and the Matabelis of Tierra del Fuego ran after him shouting, Man on a snake! but even with their strong lungs they couldn't catch him, and the cyclists pressed on to Warsaw, with Krula coming in first at only twenty-two, the age I was when I stood in Prostějov before the spread-eagle sign of Weinlich & Sons, Purveyor to the Court, Weinlich, a Jew with a gold pince-nez, impeccably dressed and scented, a book under his arm and a Havana between his lips, it was like entering a university, his sales representatives Fogl and Vertsberger had an academic aura about them too, and I stood before them with a pair of shoes in my hands as if I were in court, Did you make those shoes yourself? Weinlich asked, How many dozen can you make in a week? and I said, Two dozen, and they ran up to congratulate me and ran to get me my kidskin and box calf and told me to run and catch my train, and I left the way the triumphant yet modest Montgomery left To-bruk, the honor of being employed by a purveyor to the court, it's like working with a man who has the Order of Labor, a purveyor to the court had medals and a spread eagle on his sign, Kafka and Dvořák made the emperor's clothes and shoes, the archduke's too, and Vymětal and Po-pelka were his master butchers, the hams they had in their windows and spruce boughs and aspara-gus, a friend of mine was known for his fine frock coats, and once I invited his brother for a rest in our country air, but he got so drunk on slivovitz that he would have died if we hadn't wrapped him in curd cheese compresses, anyway he worked for the Court Purveyor Kafka who had green trousers and gold medals on his sign, and once General von Wucherer had Kafka make him a light blue coat for Corpus Christi, but the gold collar didn't fit, and his wife, the Frau Generalin, a beast like Maria Theresa, went to complain, but old man Kafka, who had the nerves of a composer, grabbed her and swept out the entrance hall with her, yelling, If it fit thousands before him, it'll fit your Freiherr too, now you know why I make so many trips to the cemetery, and what do I see but young men dozing among the tombstones instead of doing their jobs, and here I am pushing seventy and having the time of my life with you like the emperor with that Schratt lady, promising you red leather pumps like the ones I once made for Doctor Karafiát's sister, who was a beauty, but had one glass eye, which is a problem, because you never know what it's

going to do next, a hatter from Prostějov once
told me he took a woman with a glass eye to the
pictures and she sneezed and it flew out and during the break they had to go crawling under the
seats for it, but she found it and wiped it off,
pulled up her eyelid, and pop! in it went, by the
way, baking is as much of an art as shoemaking,
my brother Adolf was a trained baker, you slide
the shovel into the oven like it's a billiard cue,
and if the inspector catches you licking your fingers when you're making rolls you'll get a bop
on the beezer, and every time a baker does number one he's got to wash his hands, while a shoemaker can pick his nose all day if he likes, a
butcher has to watch himself as well, we had one
in our platoon by the name of Kocourek, Miro-
slav Kocourek, and this Kocourek had a bandaged
finger, and one day he was stuffing liverwursts
and the bandage disappeared into one of them,
and because chances were an enlisted man would
get the one with the bandage he forgot about it,

but guess what, young ladies, it was the doctor!
that's right, he was on his third liverwurst, and
the minute he cut into it he recognized his hand-
iwork and puked and Kocourek was sent to the
front, but did he die there? no, he turned hero
and won all kinds of medals, I spent some time
pushing goats tied together in a wheelbarrow to
the butcher's, and one day two little kids gam-
boled along next to me and the goats kept licking
my hands, and when I stopped in a field to rest,
the kids started licking my hands, and I wept bitter tears, what was I doing with a butcher? me,
an admirer of the European Renaissance, besides,
my stomach was all tied up in knots and it was a
miracle I hadn't ripped myself open with the
paring knife, so I switched from shoemaking to
brewing and trained as a maltster and set off on
a tour of Hungary, oh what a brewery they have
in Sopron! bright red with white trimming and
green windows, Tyrol style, nothing but white
tile inside, and nice little ladders at every window

so in case of fire the firemen can climb up and
down like the monkeys in Dresden, and Buda-
pest! what a place! one street all white with red
windows, the next all green with yellow windows, blue streets and gold streets and speckled
streets, all through the war they had bread white
as buns, their Admiral Horthy ordered the sailors
led by Matoušek to be executed, he had the poor
men blindfolded, there'd been an uprising, or mu-
tiny, as it's called, for beer, dear ladies, the barley
must be nice and clean, you don't want it sprout-
ing too soon now, do you, then you soak it in
lukewarm water and it goes to the malting floor,
where it's turned over and over with a wooden
shovel and starts putting out shoots, and from
there it goes to the kiln to dry in the fire, then
into drums, where the malt—there are Munich
malts for dark beer and Pilsen malts for light
beer—is separated from the flower, the blossoms,
that is, which make excellent cattle feed, and after
the malt has cooked for several hours in the

brewing room, it's mashed three times to maxi-
mize the sugar content, and in go the hops, which
give it that bitter flavor, and then it all goes into
vats in a special fermentation room where the
yeast is added, ordinary beer takes a month to
ferment, lager three months, some memory I've
got, eh? you won't find many more like it, the
yeast forms foamy ripples on lager, and before the
beer is barreled or bottled the foam is scooped up
in a tin pot and poured in small quantities into
each receptacle to give it that spark, that sparkle,
Munich beers can take up to six months, and
when the time comes to broach a barrel the president himself puts in an appearance, I once knew
a seamstress named Husáková, I gave her lessons,
sexual hygiene and art, and I told her the main
thing is to fill in the chinks, and she tried to get
me to run into the woods and fill hers, but I said
anyone can do that, what counts is doing something that didn't exist before, but women bring
everything back to the here and now, one day the

owner of a restaurant complained to me that his customers would erase the marks he made on the coaster to keep track of how many beers they'd ordered, and the beautiful woman at my side said, I've got a mark no one can erase, gentlemen, though of course lagers spend a full six months in the barrel, sweet Pardubice Porter has an 18 percent alcohol content just like our Nusle Senator, Brno Dragon has 14 percent like Bráník Special and Budějovice Crystal, oh dear ladies, that heady sparkle, those bitter Pilsners, the Cardinals and semisweet brews they serve at U Fleků and U Tomáše's, why will no one see that progress may be good for making people people, but for bread and butter and beer it's the plague, they've got to slow down their damn technology, in the good old breweries they made a log fire under a copper kettle and the flame traveled up through the copper and caramelized the beer—what a memory I have! a true joy—and the rye they made bread out of would rest in the barns until

November came and the whole ear went into the grain and only then did they thresh it, that was some bread, let me tell you, God's gift to man, you could smell it being baked for miles around, the older the better, which is why the emperor liked his landau more than his motorcar, liked his wine too and died on the toilet, and you should have seen him do the European Renaissance with the Schratt lady, I was on guard duty in Meidling and I saw it all, the Schratt lady standing on a ladder picking plums and the emperor holding the ladder for her and peeking up her skirt like Goethe, which goes to show how right Batista was when he said that the best safeguard of marital bliss is a well-developed body, the emperor liked to wear a Kaiserrock, a kaiser coat, this long, dark frock coat buttoned all the way up the front, a noble family if there ever was one, the emperor's, but they had the same troubles all families have, his son, the crown prince, was forced to marry Princess Stephanie of Belgium, but he was wild for Vetsera's body, she had these gigantic breasts and eyes, and it ended in a gigantic shooting match, Dáša, who works in the pharmacy and has problems with sexual hygiene, Dáša said to me when I told her about the emperor's family tragedy she said, Listen, if you and I were a couple and you started running after that slut I'd have shot you dead too, yes, tragedy rules the world and writers always have something to write about, one day I was walking along the tracks and a railway man came riding up on his bike and when he saw me he jumped down and said, Tell me the truth, Jirka, they didn't make that goal yesterday, did they? and I said, No, they didn't, and then he put one foot on the pedal and just before swinging the other one over he turned and called, Thank you, thank you, the truth prevails, I always knew you were a man of character! people keep mixing me up with referees and film stars and I've never played soccer in my life, well, only for fun, Mozart and Goethe they never played soccer either, or the emperor for that matter, no, he went chamois hunting in Ischl and wore lederhosen, you know, the little-boy shorts with the drawbridge in front, he liked people and pork, he made only one currency reform during his entire regime, and he had Šlosarek and Hugo Schenk strung up and gave my mother a twenty-five-gulden bonus, whenever she stamped cabbage, my mother, she wore white socks, we were on maneuvers with the emperor's Uncle Albrecht, the one with the buck teeth, and the emperor made the man who put up Uncle Albrecht and him during the maneuvers, Kolář his name was, the emperor made him a nobleman for his hospitality, and this Baron Kolář was so grateful he put up a monument to the emperor in front of his house, Mother and me we went out for wood one day, the soldiers were busy with their horses or eating out of cans, and we brought in two wheelbarrows of logs and two of grass for the cow, who was plug-ugly but gave us fifteen

calves, the whole street came to us for milk and
when that cow died the whole street mourned
her, but she'd left behind one last calf and we
brought the calf into the house and bottle-fed it,
every morning in came the calf to lick our faces,
my brother Adolf liked to say it came to shave
us, and when the calf grew up into a cow old man
Zpurný said he'd never seen so fine an animal in
all his born days, the only problem being that she
went berserk if she saw a train or even a bicycle,
so we had to put blinkers on her, for a thousand
years the Church has been squawking at us
Czechs to curb our passions, but how can you
make a dent in a nation when its every member
reacts according to the Batista book about safe-
guards of marital bliss, which says that shivers
run down a man's spine whenever he sees a beautiful woman and his first thought is how to get
her, as Bondy the poet says, from the vertical to
the horizontal, and he ought to know, because he
may be a poet but he's pushing two offspring in

a baby buggy everywhere he goes, my mother, now, she was a saint, she brought us up all by herself and all on beets, she was what nowadays they call a shockworker, she'd haul water from the stream when the weather was dry, but even though her beets were big as buckets, they couldn't hold a candle to Haná beets, when those damn Haná farmers left their fields there wasn't a footprint left, there was a man named Mýtný known for huge harvests, he'd been a corporal in the Uhlans and had a beard like Elijah, in summer he tucked it into his fly, in winter he wore it like a scarf, and how he would slave, first a full day's work in the woods, then a break for prayer, then chasing women and cows in the fields, egging them on with his example and his whip, what the president wouldn't give to have two hundred thousand Mýtnýs! oh and his wife ran a pub, but she poured more for herself than she did for the customers, so good Catholic that he was he beat her and beat her until one day he beat her dead, as it says in the Old Testament, and it goes without saying his cows and horses were spotless, his coffers full, and his bankbooks in order, an old woman by the name of Šumplica once used her bare feet to make a pile of the potatoes she'd dug up so she wouldn't have to bend and carry them, but old man Mýtný caught her at it and whipped the living daylights out of her and then went home and mended his clodhoppers and read a lofty book or two, before he put in his seeds he would soak them in blue vitriol, he got a kick out of slaughtering hogs and would season his soup with an African spice, by the way, young ladies, Javanese cinnamon is better than Ceylonese, cinnamon is good in mulled wine and fruit fillings, but people could be terribly behind the times during the monarchy, a peasant hoeing in the field once took his thumb for a grub and hacked it off, and a teacher by the name of Látal would flog his pupils or beat their heads against the blackboard because they couldn't get their geometry figures straight, and Zbořil, our priest, would grab boys by the scruff of the neck and shake them like rabbits because they couldn't get it into their heads that grace is inherent in God's nature and a gift from on high, he had to pray all the time and ask God to keep his temper in check, otherwise he'd forget the chalice and box the servers' ears and that was the end of the Mass, that was your Austrian discipline, all pomp and circumstance, the archbishop wore a purple biretta and purple cloak, and General Lukas had a gold collar and three stars on a field of red silk, and all a soldier had to say was I've had enough of this damn war! and he'd hang from the nearest tree, you could buy the Son of Man for thirty gulden, while a sultan paid a hundred thousand and more for his beauties, a celebrity like Saint Peter would hang upside down on the cross, while the pope, his successor, has free rein of the Lateran and Vatican, which have so many rooms he needs a guidebook to keep from getting lost, and don't think

he talks to his cardinals about the benefits of
brotherly love, no, it's all currencies and Catholic
charities, what I'm giving you now, young ladies,
are like windows on the world, points, goals,
scores, the principle the late Strauss applied to his
heavenly melodies, sending them out into the
world to refine the emotions, like the European
Renaissance, for which Themistocles and Mil-
tiades and Socrates and Goethe and Mozart did
so much and which has made it impossible for us
to say to a beauty we're tired of, Get lost, or even
Adieu, because our refined emotions require us
to compose a farewell melody or poem to be dis-
patched with a bouquet of roses, why, even the
dreams of the romantic swain are refined, if he
dreams of the trots, say, it means success in society, and if he dreams of his wife's death it means
a secret wish fulfilled, a stove fitter apprentice
once burst into tears when he was apprenticed to
a young lady on the billiard table, but another
time the bar ladies were a great help, there was

this boy who wasn't quite all there and the first
time he felt the urge he cried out, Mama, Mama,
what's happening to me! and his mother grabbed
a hundred-crown note and ran for a bar beauty,
but the boy kept falling off her so his mother had
to stick around, and she barely had time to take
a breather before he started shouting, Mama,
Mama, what's happening to me! again, but I always kept in shape like Conar Tolnes and saved
my magic hands for what we called contessa
shoes, shoes for princesses, actresses, and great
beauties, wooden heels and brass tacks, clean
work, God's own work, silver kid and yellow kid,
canary yellow, and gum dragon to make the soles
white, in the days of the monarchy shoemaking
was more chemistry than craft, today it's all
conveyor belts, I was a shoemaker, but I wore a
pince-nez and carried a stick with a silver mount-
ing because back then everyone wanted to look
like a composer or a poet, today it's the other way
round, writers have their pictures taken to look

like tramps, I once saw an American writer, a
monster, dear lady, another Count Zelikowski,
who was known for his cruelty, then there's that
man who painted the dove of peace, look at him,
a regular Mariazell beggar, your artists today they
all brush their hair into their eyes like the inmates
of the monarchy's poorhouses or a peasant sent
out to pasture, when I was young if you had two
years of schooling you had your hair permed and
combed out like a girl's so the ladies would think
you wrote poetry, and if you had three you didn't
go out in the sun any more than you had to,
whereas now even presidents tan, back in the
monarchy workers had their pictures taken with
one elbow perched on a table and eyes gazing into
the distance like Edison, whereas now they have
them taken chopping wood, and star anise, which
comes from a Chinese tree, was all the rage and
terrific in liqueurs and cakes, there were plenty of
beggars but plenty of style, Hungarian flour the
color of sand had three red hearts on its sacks,

American pastry flour had three crossed ears of grain and a Canadian with a scythe in his hand, the Archbishop Prince Eugen, commander of the Deutschmeister and member of the Apostolic Order, was the biggest swine of all the Habsburgs, he was over seven foot tall, and when his adjutant brought him his greatcoat he had to drag it on the ground, old man Grulešek read love stories as he mended sacks, and Zbořil, our priest, read the pastoral letter concerning immoral books and periodicals from the pulpit, and old man Grepl, who delivered fabrics to Olomouc, put his legs in cold water to keep from falling asleep because he had no alarm clock, in winter he went out foraging for firewood with the devil's own chains over his shoulder, he'd bang his wife's head against a beam to knock some sense into her, and she'd pray all night for God to come and empty a cartload of wood on top of him, which must be why Bondy the poet says that real poetry must hurt, as if you'd forgotten you wrapped a razor blade in your handkerchief and you blow your nose, no book worth its salt is meant to put you to sleep, it's meant to make you jump out of bed in your underwear and run and beat the author's brains out, of course in the days of the monarchy a man was responsible for his wife's soul before God, so when Tónek Opletalů stuck a knife into Ferdoška's head during an argument they were having over which of them would go to heaven he said to his wife, You vowed at the altar to obey me, and slapped her a few times as a down payment on slaps to come, my master was a good man, but he did like the bottle, and when he could afford it he'd knock back a liter of brandy in the morning and another in the afternoon and another at night, nowadays people would go crazy or rise up in arms if they had to work till midnight the way they did in the days of the monarchy, Why do you always stop me, you whore? he'd say to the wife at night, I don't stop you from smoking your china dragoon pipe, do I? and whack! he'd

smack her with his last, though you can't deny it,
people found time for fun back then too, one day
my father met a man as lazy as himself, Trávníček
was his name, and off they went to Fidler's for a
bottle of rye, schnapps came in bottles the shape
of lamp cylinders back then, anyway, my dad and
this Trávníček fellow climbed the cemetery wall
and since they'd read their Havlíček and their il-
lustrated weeklies they were so upset about the
world situation that they didn't go to work and
just sat there talking subversive talk about social
injustice, and soon they were tipsy and singing
Walking through the Woods to the Meadow One
Day and the priest flew out of the church holding
a handkerchief as big as a table napkin and shouting, Damn you, Trávníček! you're ruining my
Mass, go into the woods or I'll have you arrested,
but Papa and Trávníček kept up their singing and
before they knew it there was a cop with a feather
in his cap who told them to disperse in the name
of the law, so they did, and Papa went and bought

one of those all-day suckers to cover up his
breath, but Mama smelled it anyway and took a
rope and beat the living daylights out of him, if
you're going to hit the bottle you need to lay in
a reserve or you'll go off your rocker, though
Loja Továrků he went off his on account of the
cobblestones in the town square or maybe on account of his son's trial-run children with the town
girls, in any case he kept banging his head against
the wall and singing Oh My God Joseph, Oh My
God Joseph, and when his brain fever started
soaring he switched to All the Devils Are Set
Free, All Are Exorcizèd, after a while people noticed something was wrong and put him into an
asylum, but otherwise he was a decent fellow, he
served on the town council with Bechyně and
headed the local Sokol group, it was just those
cobblestones that got to him, or maybe his
daughter too, who once gave a man the greatest
proof of love and when the consequences started
to show blew her brains out with the gun that

hung on their wall, so you see, young ladies, people are still unenlightened and inclined to tragedy,
and if they tell the truth they seem to be lying,
the truth will out, all right, but always too late, a
beautiful girl with a classical education once married this stinking rich man because she'd read The
Foundry Owner, but she kept a locksmith's son
on the side, and one day her husband came home
and found her in the tub with the locksmith's son
and boxed his ears so hard he never heard another
word, which is why Batista's book on sexual hygiene warns men against giving in to their passions, no more than three times an afternoon
or four times for Catholics, to prevent sinful
thoughts from taking shape, you never know
where they might lead, they get into your blood,
sultans are particularly susceptible and always
come to grief, sometimes even popes and kings
have their problems and it's all over before you
know it, a kingdom on its head over a beautiful
woman, yes, but it's no use crying over spilled

milk, Mama was the one who told me, Mama was the one who warned me, women react only to feelings so you've got to lie, the wedding, the fun and games, that's the easy part, but a whole life? a butcher once told me, he said, Marriage is like dragging a cow hide along a sheet of thin ice, there are days when a wife says to her husband, You know what you need, Papa? you need a good smack in the kisser and he says to her, Mama, you dirty bitch, if you get plastered once more I'll tear your mouth open with a cramp iron, and then, young ladies, ideals start to crumble, even Goethe had his troubles, to say nothing of Mozart, oh, it's nice enough when two young people rush up to each other and clasp hands and whatever else there is to clasp, though that kind of thing is more exciting to clothed nations, naked nations are less lecherous, there's less pickpocketing too no matter how the priests go on about them, Charles IV went through four beauties and if he hadn't caught pneumonia and died he'd certainly have

gone for a fifth, he had a real eye for the ladies,
you've got to be able to tell true passion from
passing fancy, the way Batista describes them in
his book, one woman has twenty-two children
and another can have a brewery chimney fall on
her and no go, the man's got to have a regulation
sexual organ, it's right there in the dream book,
dreaming of a large organ means dignity, like
Šoupal in our town, him and his wife would drink
and pull each other's hair on the stairs, but the
minute they hit the street they were proper as
could be, at home he'd scream and yell, Let me
smell your breath, you reek of alcohol, and she'd
kneel down and plead, But all I had was a rum
chocolate, and he'd give her a few good slaps,
people have it better nowadays, but when it
comes to this kind of thing it's still the same old
story, sometimes *he* hangs himself, sometimes
she, there was a man named Kaura living behind
the station who stole by night and mended shoes
by day, he had a German wife, but she couldn't

steal worth a damn and he was so ashamed he strung himself up on a beam in the attic, or Chytil! his wife went from house to house selling shirts and pilfering all the while and when the cops brought her home he was so ashamed he had no choice but to hang himself, or that dandy Korec who worked in the health insurance office and had a son studying in Olomouc, one day Doctor Karafiát went to him and said, People are complaining they don't get their insurance payments, how do you explain that? and Korec owned up, he'd been taking the money and sending it to his son for his studies, and the doctor said it was no concern of his, though he understood, and Korec, a scapegoat of the monarchy if there ever was one, took a scythe and a liter of rum and went behind the barn and slit his throat, nowadays it's the other way around, the children study free of charge and the fathers are ready to slit their throats because those brats get more money than they do, on the other hand in the days of the monarchy you wouldn't dream of serving beef broth without a wonderful spice from Asia Minor called saffron, my cousin was a twin and a real card, he was christened Vincek and his brother was christened Ludvíček, and when they were a year old their mother was bathing them in a tub and popped out to a see a neighbor, and when she got back half an hour later one of them had drowned, and they were so much alike nobody could tell which one, Ludvíček or Vincek, so they flipped a coin, heads for Ludvíček, tails for Vin-cek, and it came up Ludvíček, but when my cousin Vincek grew up he began to wonder—and he had plenty of time for it, he was always out of a job—he began to wonder who really did drown, whether the person walking around on earth wasn't really Ludvíček and he, Vincek, was up in heaven, which led him to drink and to wan-der along the water's edge and go in swimming, testing the waters, so to speak, till at last he drowned, by way of proof that he hadn't been the one to drown back then, but also because back then people had to look for work, while today work looks for people, so they don't have time to get into trouble, which I realized when Bondy the poet wheeled his two babies into the pub and quoted Socrates as saying that prostitution is employment for the unemployed, one day Tóneček from the coffee house offered us a few salamis if we'd break some stones for him, and we were hacking away and hacking away when suddenly a dark cloud covered the sun and it was black as night and thunder roared and lightning flashed and we had to take cover in a ditch, but just as suddenly the sun came out, and when we got home that evening Mama said, You'll never guess what happened, boys, Karásek hanged himself in the woods while you were there breaking your stones, it was because his girl went with other men, young ladies, I was always careful about that sort of thing, the shoemaker I worked for had a daughter, Mařena her name was, with a

stomach like a stein, a backside like a barn, and a
chest like Maria Theresa's, and one day they made
me sleep over and bedded me down next to the
stove, and when morning came I felt Mařena
stroking my face and rubbing her chest against
mine, but I gave such a start—even then I was as
sensitive as a Saxon prince—that I banged my
head against the stove and had to dip it in the
bucket to wash away the blood, and the whole
family jumped out of bed and cheered and wanted
me to name the day but I refused, I told them
that like Goethe I had a weak heart and was more
inclined to poetry, which slowed them down for
a while, but then Mařena bought me a tie and a
ring made of nickel, so I used a tip from Batista's
book on how to have a happy marriage and made
believe I was thinking about music, so Mařenka
married a man named Jetrudka who made her six
children and poor, he was drunk all the time and
if he so much as sneezed in her direction she got
pregnant, three of her children went crazy, and

when the other three got old enough to think for themselves they stuck their heads in the noose, so much for Anna Nováková's dream book, which says, dreaming of an infant means pleasure in the offing! well, maybe for a bigwig with a big house, but a baby crying is no pleasure, the monarchy was big on pomp, but when you went out walking you couldn't help tripping over beggars' peglegs and instead of enjoying the women's bosoms I'd worry about their woes, one day I was walking along minding my own business when I noticed a Jewish beauty with a nose like a train hook sitting on the border between two fields, waiting for the first Saturday star to come out, and because she had no panties on I had one eye glued to the spot where Goethe liked to look before he sat down to write his poems, and I went over and introduced myself and we immediately struck up an intimate conversation, she told me how she could ride a bicycle no hands, which was really revolutionary at the time, and I told her about a policeman who'd dug up a public hygiene regulation and used it as an excuse to go and bathe gypsy girls fifteen and under, he'd order the gypsy elders to heat up the water, then shoo them away, take off his coat, roll up his sleeves, and go to, but one day the police chief peeked through the keyhole as the policeman carried out the public hygiene regulation and the policeman landed in court, after which the police chief took over washing the gypsy girls and the gypsy women couldn't understand why he didn't wash *them* too, anyway, the Jewish beauty sitting and waiting for the first Saturday star to come out blushed bright red and whispered to me, I'm not as pure as I might be either, so I was a hero once more, I went with an embezzler's daughter too, not many men can claim that, her name was Helenka, the embezzler's daughter, and we played Diabolo together, and each time she leaned forward to discard I looked down her blouse, she had such beautiful breasts that for years I would stutter and make spelling mistakes at the thought of them, so I followed Christ's example and kept my illusions, I went with beauties but didn't let them get too close, thus preserving my freedom, like Doctor Karafiát, who shuddered at the thought of even dreaming about a woman in her underwear, which writers find shocking too and they're used to all sorts of things, the embezzler father of the beauty in question tried to get me to work for him, but I knew he had two sons, slick dressers both of them, pince-nez and all, one was caught misappropriating funds and, as was the fashion in those days, put a Browning to his head, only the ruling class used Brownings for the purpose, and the other had a wife whose name was Nina, a giant of a woman who wore nothing but satin and drank nothing but rosolio, and one day when she was drawing water from the well she lost her balance and fell in and they didn't find her for a week because they thought, as was the fashion in those days, that she had been carried off by a student,

and by then she was all puffed up and ugly,
Mother of God, isn't life breathtakingly beautiful!
another reason I refused to become part of their
family was that their uncle was a religious fanatic,
the kind that goes around kissing the ground because he so loved God's hills and dales and tearing down fences because heaven has no fences so
why do we need them on earth, he was one of
the first to call for boundary strips between farms
to be plowed under, he would kneel down in the
public square and cry out that love would tear
down all fences between people, but people took
it the wrong way and ran home and lay down
with one another on their sofas, and so the man
went and hanged himself on his mother's cross in
the cemetery, and the local priest was furious because he had to reconsecrate the whole place, I
was always surprised to read in Anna Nováková's
dream book that hanging yourself in church
means you will become a church dignitary because suicides have to be buried at night, hush-

hush, off to the side somewhere, like the wife of the army doctor, the notary's son, she was a jewel she was, just like you, young ladies, when she came to us for milk she'd say to me, How about popping round for a visit? she said I was the spitting image of the late Strauss in his youth, her mother came from a castle just beyond Přemyšlovice, it was called Hlochov and it belonged to Bochner, and her father, who was also a notary, rode around in a coach that was drawn by four white horses and had six spotted mastiffs with their tongues out running behind, and the other notary's son he wore a sky blue jacket and black trousers with a red silk stripe down the side, no army could hold a candle to ours when it came to looks, your soldiers today they're a bunch of sad sacks compared with us, our waists laced in like the ladies', and when we came home on leave the ladies would piss olive oil they were so jealous of our corsets, every member of the medical corps had two rows of buttons, gold buttons, and a gold

collar, silk-lined, and the head doctor wore special braiding and a collar made entirely of gold,
magnificent, the only possible competition would
be nature wanting to show what it could do and
coming up with another kingfisher or parrot, but
besides pomp and beggars the monarchy was big
on discipline, it drove the soldiers up the wall, the
torture, the beatings, the prisons and chains, a
regular concentration camp it was, but the army
doctor, the notary's son, he was as proud as
proud could be, he went to war the way beauties
go on walks, but then the most terrible thing happened, one soldier murdered another for the
money his mother sent to him, and the murderer
poured a whole bottle of brandy down the corpse's
throat to make it look like he was drunk, and
the doctor thought he was and gave the body a
kick, but another soldier saw the murderer do it
and turned him in, and they threw him in jail,
and he strung himself up with a towel, and at the
funeral his mother nearly cracked the church

open with her wailing, but she paid what had to
be paid and he was buried in the churchyard even
though he'd committed suicide, only they had to
do it at night, hush-hush, off to the side, whereas
when they bury you at the front, young ladies,
they toss you anywhere and you're gone for
good, like a lost handkerchief, and would you believe it? Anna Nováková says in her dream book,
holding a dead man's watch means a wedding and
being locked up in an insane asylum means a great
fortune awaits you! but you'll never guess what
happened to our stationmaster, who raised turkeys and was always worried his assistant would
forget to switch the tracks for the express train
and always went himself and checked, well, one
day the express train ran into a whole flock of his
turkeys, that was a sight, let me tell you, you
know how express trains speed along so fast they
blow bits of paper and twigs behind them, well,
this one was all turkey parts, and the assistant
stationmaster at the next station got three thighs

on his head and the stationmaster at the station after that thought he'd had a featherbed emptied on him, those express trains are really something when they barrel through a station, the Libice stationmaster had his application for promotion torn out of his hand and couldn't put on his new uniform for two whole weeks until they finally found the application five stations away, then there was the woman on her way home from a pig feast who walked along the tracks to save time, and when the train ran over her it dragged her soup bucket to the next station and splashed the stationmaster with barley, then there are the people who sit next to the tracks in their little huts in the middle of the fields and crank the barriers up and down, you can't even see them at night, but they're there, shining their boots and brushing off their uniforms and standing at the barrier, saluting, the express train rushing into the night, covering them with dust, streaking them with mud, but there they stand at attention sa-

luting it, the last remnants of the monarchy, those
people, the monarchy had its Lukases, who made
garrison inspections without beatings or even
punishments, and its Zelikowskis, who were first-
class swine, Zelikowski not only beat his men, he
had them tied to trees, officers mostly, so they'd
know how things were supposed to look when
he rode along and the troops had to go into columns or echelon formation or single or double
file or form a square or poof! disperse like spar-
rows when you shoot at them and then come
back together cheek by jowl on command, the
officers had to know what he meant when he
raised his saber to the sky because a general can't
go shouting to sixteen companies, an orchestra
conductor doesn't shout at his musicians, Hey,
you there, didn't you see that hold? no, he's got
a baton, and it's not for whipping, it's for con-
ducting, giving signals, though of course a general
has to think about winning a battle and losing as
few men as possible, they tried to promote me to

corporal, but I refused, they keep putting you on guard duty or sending you out on patrols, you have to go to classes at the edge of the woods, where they draw all over blackboards and the lieutenants shout, NCO front and center! and you've even got to ask permission to do number one, and when you get to the front you start seeing all these unmistakable signs, the ammunition, the grenades, the wounded, one soldier got the trots, also known as diarrhea, from the water, some memory I've got, eh, young ladies? there he was, crouching in a trench with his belt round his neck, and who should swing down from his horse but General Zelikowski shouting what a shithouse regiment they'd given him, shithead sons of bitches all of them! and he took his sword and gave the soldier a good whack on the back, I got to know the front like the back of my hand, the pandemonium, the men stabbing one another blindly, by mistake, too weak to stop, anything to keep the enemy from digging in, the officers

on pins and needles, whole platoons wallowing
in blood, horses and all, everything burning,
trees flying through the air, orderlies piling the
wounded on horses to take them off to the
woods, and not a woman in sight, they weren't
allowed at the front, they stayed behind in the
brothels of Przemyśl and Cracow, there were
windows in the brothel doors and I'd peek in, one
young lady once opened the door and said, Do
anything for you, soldier boy? some of them did
it for a loaf of bread, but Lieutenant Hovorka
told us we'd be better off with nonprofessionals,
it took a few chocolates, but then it was true love,
I found a schoolmaster's daughter who would do
it for a nice white roll, but all I had was our army
bread, so she kissed my hand and in exchange I
told her about the time I spent in Split guarding
an old freight car filled to the brim with ecrasite,
which they used to blow up bridges and which
looked like flypaper or a powder you buy at the
pharmacy, and then I read her excerpts from the

dream book, chatting with a young lady means a rash business venture, frolicking with a hussy at night means beware of beguiling words, and then I told the schoolmaster's daughter in my best Polish that the young miss was pleasing to the eye and she told me that the young master was too and she hoped the shooting would soon cease, I was always the gentleman, which is why I was in correspondence with Europe's finest beauties, in Ziegenhals I won the heart of an industrialist's daughter, she wore a blue dress and a yellow veil and once, when I was rowing her across a lake in the woods and singing Mein Herz, das ist ein Bienenhaus, the boat started sinking, but I saved her because the lake was shallow, Anna Hering her name was and she wrote me pink love notes, our whole town was abuzz with who I was writing to, once she sent me a bottle of May Magic perfume that smelled like lily of the valley, I was trying to get out of the army by smoking cigars dipped in saffron, you had to be very careful not to let your fingers turn yellow so I'd bite them till they bled, which is in the same category as beguiling a beautiful woman, charming her with words, but as our late mayor used to say when he came into the bar to see whether the beauties there had beautiful calves, Anyone can get it for money, it takes a real virtuoso like you to pull it off free of charge, so I was a hero once more, because I went at it like the officers, Men, Lieutenant Hovorka used to say, you've got to go about it with kid gloves, think of it more like sharpening a pencil than thrusting a bayonet, so I never said much, I just watched to see what little vices my beauties might have and they would out by themselves, I like cigarettes and wine, she'd say, and I'd say, Well, I don't, and she'd say, And what *do* you like? and I'd say, Beautiful women, I'd say, and she'd squeal, Oh you devil you, and throw a shoe at me, once I had the honor of riding all the way to the Haubitz barracks on Iduna, the general's mare, a real beauty, a rich brown with a white star on her forehead like a movie star, a star like the hole you shoot through a handkerchief, but as we were sailing along, me and Iduna, we ran into an old woman and she turned such a somersault that I was worried Iduna had done her some harm, I didn't want the general to have to court-martial me, after all, but on we flew across Olomouc, and Iduna leaped through the barracks fence—it's a good thing I kept my head close to her mane, I barely had time to duck—and into the stable, and when I went to the canteen for some raspberry juice, I found a pretty girl working there, Cílka was her name, and she started dancing with me, and her boss got jealous and said Cílka, go and do your work in the kitchen! and pressed up to me herself, meanwhile Cílka stood in the doorway polishing knives and showing me behind her boss's back how she would stab her if she could, and her boss said to me, You're really temperamental, you know that, soldier? so I told her that if she dreamed of catching a pheasant then love would soon find a place in her heart, and she slipped a pack of Egypts into my pocket and asked me to go on, and while Cílka showed me more and more new ways of doing her in I told her that a well-heated room means the love of a man for a woman, and when she started squirming I leaned over and whispered, But the most wonderful dream of all is when two oxen butt each other, because that means true bliss in love, and added, for which I paid dearly, I caught an ugly disease and had to go to Brzadín for treatment, and as she made to move away she tried to reach into my pocket for the Egypts, but I said to her, No, you don't, I said, given's as good as gone, which she had to accept, she even gave me a schnapps for the road and thanked me for being so kind as to warn her, because she'd had one of those diseases, once I took a milkmaid to the Urania in the upper square, they were doing this Jewish play about the troubles of a man named Ahasuerus,

and the milkmaid kept licking my ear and asking
me to marry her, and I said I would, though I
hadn't finished my stint in the army yet and had
a weak heart and couldn't stop dreaming about
canaries in cages, which according to Anna Nováková meant I would always long for freedom,
and she whispered, Wow, what a catch you'd
make! and her hair smelled of milk and vanilla,
but three days later I was off to Dalmatia and the
sea, you should have seen the storm that came up,
when nature goes wild like that and gets into a
man's pants it's enough to turn him into a poet,
waves as big as our house, a boat hurled up onto
the road, and boulders tumbling down from the
cliffs, overturning trains, sweeping men and mules
into the sea on their way back from the vineyards,
columns of water tall as towers, and near starva-
tion for us soldiers, Mother of God! the rotten
fish we ate, morale fell so low we actually went
begging, the sign over the barracks read VOJARNA
KRALJA JUSUPA, King Joseph's Barracks, all in

gold, but a first lieutenant scratched out the corn kettle, a first lieutenant! if General Zelikowski had seen that he'd have pulled out his crop and given it to him, a dandy of a Jew gave me a gulden to shine up his belt and his gun for him, he was going into town to establish some international relations, as he put it, but along came our beast of a Sergeant Brčul, six and a half feet of bad blood, and said, Where's the Jew boy? Went to town, I said, well, the Serge he starts cursing— Jebem ti boga! Kurac na drobno!—because Freiherr von Wucherer had expressly forbidden soldiers from going on rampages in town, so he comes and lies down in the Jew's bed and when the Jew staggers back after midnight, totally beat, Brčul leaps up, knocks him down, kicks him all over the floor in his special uniform, and sends him out on guard duty, and when I went out to relieve him I found him swinging in the wind, hanging from a tree in a corner of the courtyard, strung up by his own hand and shiny belt, nobody appreciates that kind of thing anymore, when I told the story to some truck drivers in Libeň they just laughed, one Saturday afternoon they were racing 111's along Breakneck Hill, and while they were on their way down there was this dentist going up, he'd left his umbrella at the office, and just as he was sticking his key into the door one of the 111's burst a spring and barreled smack into the office and it lurched away from his key, the whole office, and he was left standing there with his key in the air, it's a good thing Count Zelikowski didn't see that because he was known for his cruelty, while Major Mičoković he always put stones on the money when he counted out our pay so the wind wouldn't get it, he always warned us not to spend it on drink before we'd bought buttons and Vaseline and thread, the countryside was so beautiful, as romantic as Jerusalem, paths going up and up, always in need of repair though, people eating nothing but oat patties, vineyards hard as cement, I once saw a

Dalmatian woman tending sheep in a meadow, it might have been a painting except she turned to me and said, Are you single, young man? and I nodded and she came and sat next to me and pointed out who had died in which hut, but I was late for grenade practice, they had these newfangled grenades, young ladies, they looked like pears, but instead of a stem they had this string coming out of them, and the Zugsführer, the platoon leader, would use a dud to show us how to pull the string and count to twenty, but one day some smart aleck put a live one in its place while the platoon leader went to the latrine and when he came back, pow! off flew his hand and out through the window, giving Captain Tonser, who happened to be riding past, a mean slap, the same thing happened to the owner of an outdoor movie theater who had an iron hand, one day he caught some kids sitting in a tree getting a free show so he climbed up on a chair and swatted and swatted with his iron hand until the branches cracked and

fell, and when he got home he decided to give his
son a clout for good measure, but the iron hand
flew off its hinges and out through the window,
where it knocked down a policeman who was
standing there sharpening his pencil to write a
ticket, but what happened to me one day at roll
call was they called out my name among the fallen
in action, date of birth and all, and when I
shouted, Hey, I'm alive! they called me in and
gave me two weeks in the can for talking during
roll call, Man, one of the fellows said, if it'd been
me I'd have packed my things and hightailed it
out of there, I'd have gone straight home to bed
and when the war was over I'd have just crossed
my name off the war memorial, but I liked to
gaze at myself in the mirror wearing my uniform,
I looked so good in it, I was like the sun coming
out for a stroll when I stepped out in my light
blue tunic, my black trousers with red piping, my
shiny leather belt and nickel bayonet, and my
gold-rimmed shako, and I knew that the head un-

der that shako wasn't filled with straw, no, it was
jam-packed with the highest-quality gray matter
full of whorls and squiggles, just like Edison's, oh
Edison, the man who invented the machine that
made it possible for us to sit at home in our slip-
pers and enjoy the glories of the concert hall, that
is, the man who invented the phonograph, which
had never existed before, think of him sitting
there for three days, poor man, thinking of nothing but earphones, no, young ladies, not even the
most beautiful woman can rival a famous man like
that, a woman doctor in Cracow ordered me to
take off all my clothes, climbed on top of me, and,
pressing her cold ear against my heart, she said,
Why is your heart pounding so? so I told her
about the European Renaissance and how a real
man trembles like a frog about to leap whenever he sees a beautiful woman, which is why
art drives so many writers mad, especially when
they want to improve on it, their brains turn to
sawdust and no one can do a thing about it, a

composer by the name of Isvtán once tore a chandelier out of the ceiling in his grief, and when
Edison's bride came for him she found him sitting
there, thinking away, with a little glass stool under his feet to keep the earth's gravity from disturbing him, yes, that's right, and after his death
they opened up his brain and found it jam-packed
with the highest-quality gray matter, a fortune-
teller once read my cards and said that if it wasn't
for a tiny black cloud hanging over me I could
do great things and not only for my country but
for all mankind, then she reached over to me and
I fell off the rocking chair and overturned the
aquarium, and when I'd told all that to the Polish
doctor who was lying on top of me she asked,
Where are you going to take me tonight? and I
quoted her Anna Nováková, Dreaming of a gold-
finch in a cage means your lascivious ways will
bring you to a bad end, but the doctor stood up
and said, Couldn't you find something better? so
I said, Dreaming of an anniversary celebration

means unquenchable passion, and she said, A good beginning at least, and she made Turkish eyes at me, because most men's minds go straight to hanky-panky, but I take a different tack, I want to be a hero, when Marion the magician and hypnotist came to town he had to stamp his own documents, the officials were afraid he'd hypnotize them so they flew the coop the minute they saw him, I was on the stage too at the time, in The Balalaika, I wore a guardsman's uniform, the set was all doors with keyholes and I sang Many a Maiden Fair I've Kissed and then a purple spotlight came on and I sang, Sing, balalaika, the sweetest melody on earth, The one that gives me second birth, The song called I Love You, and I was a hero, I hit high C, not like your garden-variety yodelers who low like cows calving, no, I was a real tenor, another Járinek Pospíšil, I could wow the ladies as much as Marion the magician and hypnotist, if you like we can put on the play here and now, we'll cast one of you as the great tsarina, but we'll have to find some falsies, you there, you'll do, not all tsarinas were beautiful, I'll play the high priest, which means I carry a chalice, the chandelier gets shot down in the finale, no, I'd rather play the baron, though how can we get his horse on stage? what if we wind rags around its hoofs, then it won't harm the stairs, but more important, we don't want it shying when the music plays, it might fall into the orchestra, the swine dealer can be played by Ruda Turek, the first lieutenant, he's got a neck like a Swiss steer, I once tried to do splits with a beauty in the Catholic House and gave myself a hernia, which isn't so bad for a man, a man makes anything look good, but when a maiden wears a truss and a lovesick swain comes up against that cold belt, those nickel springs, his ideals start to falter and his desire to flag, Christ our Lord was once invited to a wedding where they were going overboard on the wine so he turned it into water, that was known as the miracle of Cana of Galilee, there was a time when I had the strangest dreams, handling the bones of a corpse means a great joy awaits you, it's interesting how young poets think of death while old fogies think of girls, a hunter once told me he couldn't get over how happy an old buck looked wooing a doe, if you dream of a bed of tulips it means you'll fall in love with a lovely girl and she'll never know, a certain poet by the name of Bondy once told me that people have strange ideas about what writing poetry means, they think it's like going for water with a bucket or that poets just lift up their eyes unto the heavens and the heavenly hosts rain down verses upon them, but I told him, Think of Christ our Lord, he had such a head on his shoulders that even today the professors go gaga over him, and he wasn't just God's little Favorite either, no, he was a champ, a muscleman handy with a horsewhip so he could drive those cattle traders out of the temple and tell them he came not to send peace but a sword, a saber, that is, and people still don't understand, but that's because the smart ones die and stupid ones get born in their place, some people clean latrines and others are doctors, some women lie in bed all day reading novels and others go out and do what the novels tell them about, poor Bondy gave his fingers a sniff after changing his offspring in the baby buggy in the pub and said, I sense a deep movement in its early stages, and sure enough within half an hour he was wiping one of the babies with the latest issue of Czech Word and mumbling, Christ! it's enough to get to a Korean hangman, on Corpus Christi, marching triumphant into Przemyśl, we saw a young lady lying in a ditch pointing at herself and calling out, Come and celebrate our glorious victory, but none of the soldiers could bring themselves to take her up on it because she was as ugly as the Turkish night, I never went in for that anyway, I was a different kind of hero, I liked the baronesses in sick bay and later, during the First Republic, pretty Sokol girls and nurses, one of them shaved my stomach to prepare me for an operation because the head physician told me I'd be going under the knife the next day and would I be so kind as to sign a piece of paper in case I stayed under, it was just his way of perking me up, and when my time came he put on his white cap like a pastry chef and the nurses pulled on his gloves for him like he was a baby and he was all set to dig into me when the door flies open and in comes an old lady holding a basket asking which room her husband is in because she's brought him his pork and cabbage, well, he ran up and grabbed her—he was a giant of a man with a real temper on him—and kicked her out and screamed at the janitor, How could you let her past? because he should have been elbow-deep in my blood by then, stitching up my hernia, you can't imagine how good it feels to leave the hospital and look around you, like in the song, It's a beautiful world we live in, A world by God to us given, tra la la, I had a blacksmith in my room, Bernádek his name was, who'd down a stein of beer in one gulp and if a horse put up a fuss and refused to stand for him he'd flip it over and shoe it on its side, but not even he could stop pneumonia, it spread to his stomach and he was gone before he knew what hit him, I was the only one who came out on top, a pretty nurse served me pheasant and asked me why I wasn't married, why I let so fine a body go to waste, and for an answer I slipped out from under the covers and was about to give her a dancing lesson when they chased me back to bed because after a hernia operation they make you lie there like a corpse, a giant of a girl, but beautiful, once called to me from the Elbe, Come into the water and I'll give you a kiss, so in I went—neck deep, clothes and all—and got my prize, a hero once more, back on land I had to wring out more than my clothes, I'd just picked up my pay in ten-crown notes, and there I stood in my underpants, the women rushing down to the river to have a

look at me, the whole town on its feet, yes, there
I stood like Montgomery at Tobruk, freethinkers
like to taunt the Church by asking, If Christ was
God, why did he take up with a fallen woman?
well, I say there wasn't anything he could do
about it, I can't resist the charms of a beautiful
woman, why should Christ? one of the male
beauties of his day, like Conar Tolnes, and thirty,
in the prime of life, besides, even if Mary Magdalene was nothing more than a barmaid she
gained favor in the heavens and worked her way
up to sainthood, not only did she refuse to betray
Christ, she used her hair to wipe away his blood
while the poor man hung there on the cross for
preaching social progress and all men are equal,
and when his mother fell to pieces and sobbed,
who comforted her but Mary Magdalene, think
about it, where are all the other beauties of her
day? gone and forgotten, but little Mary Magdalene will forever touch the hearts of poets, what
a fate for a handsome young man trained in the

art of carpentry, of sawing boards and beams, and boom! off he goes to teach the world that loving your neighbor doesn't mean somersaults on the sofa, it means giving help wherever help is needed, for learning my catechism I got a picture of Jesus holding the chalice, catechism was all the rage in those days, as important as political reliability and family background today, who is the Father and who is the Son and who is the Holy Spirit? one priest was taken to court because the Ulman sisters drew a blank when he asked them what the Holy Trinity was, so he sat them bare-bottomed on a hot stove and they never married, nobody wanted to have anything to do with them because they didn't know what the Holy Trinity is, not that anyone else knew, but people had to make believe they did, so the Ulman sisters started growing sunflowers, there was a wave of murders and robberies at the time, if you lived in the wilds you'd close your shutters at night and keep axes and firearms at hand, once in the dead

of night a miller heard a saw making a hole in his
door, a hole just big enough for a hand to fit
through and undo the bolt, so he stole up to the
door with his ax and the minute the hand stuck
through, thwack! he chopped it off, the police
looked and looked but couldn't find anybody
with a missing hand, the priest cursed right and
left because he had to bury the hand in the cemetery and buy a little coffin for it, Mother of God!
a soldier on sentry duty in Olomouc once spied
a fire in the cemetery, so he ran and broke into
the mortuary and what did he find but the grave-
digger standing next to a cauldron of hands and
feet in boiling fat and singing, The little hands and
little feet of the little girl I love, or once I took a
beauty of mine to a little tavern deep in the To-
mašov woods and there were nine white crosses
across the road because a fellow once lay in wait
there and then chopped up all the members of a
wedding party with his ax, I mean, the things that
happen, which is reason I have no children, why

should I want to see my line continue? who can guarantee my children will take after me? Who's going to shut your eyes when you die? the women keep asking me, but I say, Nobody dies at home anymore, the minute you start to fade, up pulls an ambulance and off you go to die behind a screen, all by yourself, relatives don't care anymore, even money's lost its charm, the best thing would be if people the world over got together and held off making babies for a spell, you trip over them everywhere you go, we could dock people's wages, fifty crowns for one child, a hundred for the second, three hundred for the third, and when they got up to five they'd lose half their salary and be given a good thrashing in the town square, it wouldn't have to go on forever, just until we could take our beauties to the woods and pay tribute to the European Renaissance without having to worry about being stared at by crowds, go camping nowadays and you sleep packed together like graves in a cemetery, a woman friend once asked me to take her dog for a walk, but instead I took it to see my beauties at the bar, where two guests pissed on it by mistake, and when I took the dog back to her she petted it, smelled her hand, and said, Where'd you take the dog anyway? he sure doesn't smell like a day in spring, dogs are all well and good, but only watchdogs, a goldsmith once beat a bulldog by mistake and that bulldog never forgot it, and one day the goldsmith was brushing the dog and it jumped up and bit him in the neck, and with the fangs still in his neck he dragged himself over to his desk and pulled out a gun, but he aimed in the mirror and missed and hit his own ear instead, nearly killed himself, and when he finally did get the dog he had to get its teeth pried open with a crowbar, another man, getting ready for a dance, was trimming his nostril hairs in the mirror and practically cut his nose off, when I cut I cut like a fiddler fiddling, with feeling, you should have seen those Przemyśl recruits off for the front, rich villages, every villager a poacher, what a sight, the mayor escorting the men to the enlistment center, the ribbons, the banners, villages ransacked for miles around, Germans herded into the brewery, the mayor knife in the neck for his pains, one false look and it was curtains, but you couldn't beat it for pomp, the cream of the Moravian nation, giants they were and hot-tempered, with two brass bands, and when they slaughtered their hogs and feasted on them the village was all decked out in flowers and streamers, spick-and-span, and there was always someone carrying their guts off in a bucket, because in the days of the monarchy men were killed right and left in pub brawls or on their way home or they ended up swinging from the rafters because they had so many children, those Przemyśl fellows once laid an ambush for me because I was flirting with one of their girls, but I swung round, pulled out my pistol and pow! pow! let them have it, they fell like flies, those giants, and I was a hero once more, like Tom Mix and his smoking revolver, then there was that uproar over Anežka Hrůzová, our people thought it was that Hilsner fellow who did it because some fool reported seeing Hilsner in the woods nearby, their star witness he was, holding his bike with one hand and doing his business with the other, so poor Hilsner was thrown in jail and Jews had to leave Polná, people even started singing a little ditty that went, Don't buy anything from Jews, Sugar, coffee, flour, Blue-eyed Anežka they killed, In her finest hour, and then Anežka's brother came out with it on his deathbed, *he'd* killed her and for the money, a policeman on patrol once stopped at a pub for a schnitzel and liked it so much he ordered a second, and after waiting and waiting for the waitress to come back he went to look for her and where did he find her but in the cellar, hacking away at her daughter, who was hanging naked on a hook, Mother of God, so he handcuffed her and booked her on the spot, that's the kind of story people liked to tell when they made their own radio and television for one another, but what I liked even better was to stroll through town in my English suit and one of those floppy-brimmed hats, oh what fun it was to window-shop, I loved the pharmacy in Olomouc with the violet-scented toilet soaps, the Lila Blanc and Violeta de Nice glycerine soaps, the extra-fine Rosa de Shiraz, once I was held up by a dragoon behind the Maria-Schnee-Kaserne, Your money or your life! he cried, a lesser man would have fainted dead away, but I pulled out my Browning and said, Clear off if you value your life, clear off or I'll shoot! when I went to visit my brother for two weeks and stayed for thirty years he gave me what he called a Mexican, which was a rifle, to protect the driving belts behind the brewery, one night I tore it off the wall and shot it at a passing policeman, you should have heard the bullets whistling and ricocheting off the bridge, I had no time to stop and ask, Who goes there? an Aus-

trian soldier must always shoot first, if he wants
to be a hero, that is, another pharmacy had hair
lotions in the window, like Cyrano, which
showed a water nymph rising out of a lake with
roses around her waist and will-o'-the-wisps or
maybe tiny stars behind her, a sight for sore eyes!
as beautiful as Mozart, once three Picek seam-
stresses were out rowing while we were working
on the brewery well, and one of them, a real
beauty, called out to me so I jumped right in,
shorts and all, and swam over to their boat, those
were our Austrian manners, even ordinary people
acted like their lives were being filmed or pho-
tographed, once when I was helping a baker de-
liver his wares in Moravian Slovakia I saw a
drunken wedding party in a church trying to pour
slivovitz down the saints' throats, and when the
priest got wind of it he stormed in like a fighter
plane and kicked and screamed and called them a
band of Tartars, Is that how you behave in God's
temple? out, the lot of you, and don't come back

until you're more sober or at least less drunk!
from there I went to Hradisko, where I worked
in a brewery, and then I made a triumphant re-
turn in a striped suit, white-knobbed cane, and
the last word in Parisian boaters, some people are
dragged home by the police looking like something the cat's dragged in, while I came home like
a movie star with a hundred gulden in my pocket,
enough to pay off all my debts and buy a cow
from Ponikve, I had the papers drawn up by old
man Tyátr, the one who turned the old theater
into a pub and whose wife had eighty cats and
did nothing all day but keep their milk bowls full,
another pharmacy had a preparation called Ka-
loderma, and a Karlsruhe firm by the name of
Wolf und Sohn kept all Moravia supplied with its
skin cream and fine pink face powder, the box
showed a dreamy-eyed woman looking out into
the distance, her hand resting on her temple and
her head wound round with a light veil, everybody was jealous of that cow from Ponikve, a

white Swiss, all white, it set me back eighty gulden, but we eventually sold it to the butcher because it was barren, of all the family my uncle
went the farthest, and he made it to Zugsführer,
platoon leader, he also wrote in a fine hand and
was awarded a gold cross by the emperor, he
wore gold braiding and a spiked helmet and was
six foot tall and when he was a bachelor he could
pull a pub to pieces like Římský from Kokory,
but he sobered up after taking a wife, he married
the head forester's daughter and built a house in
Valašsko and raised turkeys and ended up chief
of police, I once bought one of my beauties a lily-
scented cream for extra-fair skin, Steckenpferd,
from a firm in Radebeule, and for Zdenka, one of
the Havrda girls, I bought a discreetly packaged
and fully guaranteed gold-medal preparation by
the name of Sinulin, and when she asked me what
I wanted for it I said I wanted her to go for a
walk with me, and she laughed and asked why,
and I told her my hygiene manual said that a

person suffering from heat prostration—she suf-
fered from heat prostration—should rub lukewarm
water directly on the exposed chest, and she said,
Oh you men and your one-track minds! the
world is a beautiful place, don't you think? not
because it is but because I see it that way, the way
Pushkin saw it in that movie, poor Pushkin, to
die in a duel, and so young, his last poems gush-
ing from the bullet hole in his head, I could tell
from the picture that *he* admired the European
Renaissance too, he had fantastic muttonchops,
you know, the whiskers our own Franz Joseph
wore, and Strauss the composer, I was walking
along the river one day when Libuška rode up to
me on her bicycle—practically knocked me over,
in fact—and said, When are you going to bring
me another bunch of roses, another bouquet? and
for an answer I upped and kissed her, just like
Hans Albers in the steamship scene, and she
screamed, My God! and I laughed and said, Not
your God but your man, which made *her* laugh

and practically knock me over again and opened the way to another adventure, which I was man enough to take advantage of, and in another pharmacy I saw a whole row of bottles of Peru Tanin, which promised to make your hair grow long and thick and showed the two daughters of the inventor with hair down to their ankles, though in the days of the monarchy long hair was less important than big busts, there were women who had to wear rucksacks filled with bricks to keep from toppling over, they were really something those bosoms, from morning till night the monarchy thought of nothing but bosoms, the bra stuffing that went on! having a daughter with breasts smaller than beer bottles was a family tragedy, it's making a comeback now, by the way, you're starting to see the build you saw then, when I watched the Spartakiad on television I saw a pack of giants in shorts and halters hurtling across the screen, as fully packed as Maria Theresa, our girls all of them, the men were beat after

a day of watching them on parade in such num-
bers, that night I stole into a garden and picked
some roses, then I climbed the fence into Libuška's garden and left the roses on her windowsill
like the Mexicans and the Spaniards, and they do
nothing but ride horses and serenade their se-
ñoritas with guitars, and I was so diplomatic that
the next day Libuška called to me through the
curtains to come and see her, so I looked on while
she slipped out of her shoes and peeled off her
stockings, draped herself over the ottoman and
asked if she sent shivers up my spine, threw herself on the couch and sniffed the roses I'd given
her, and then, sitting up and making eyes at me,
she undid her blouse and cut into her skin with
a razor blade and said, Come and bind it, quick,
before I get blood poisoning, and while I pulled
the bandage tight she said, You don't like me as
much as you like the bar ladies, do you? and I,
ever the cavalier, put her mind at ease, You have
other charms, dear lady, I said, You are slender,

you have shapely legs, and she revived at once, so we took the wash out to the mangle, and the old women were green with envy, Wouldn't lift a finger for *us* now, would he! and I quoted Anna Nováková's dream book to her, Putting laundry through a mangle means you will soon be privy to deep secrets, and she told me how she planned to celebrate her twenty-first birthday and that she'd be scared to go to the island with me at midnight, there was something in my eyes, but I said, You'll get over it, Libuška, you're wild now, but eventually you'll be snapped up by a widower and then you'll need every trick in the book, you can't be too careful, Keep a low profile, a young wife once told me, and we'll make for the woods after dark, another of the Havrda girls, Vlasta— the one who played the piano and spoke German and did handstands on the billiard table and her skirt flopped like a poppy—Vlasta would say to me, You know what makes you so exciting? the way you ignore me, while Navrátilová whispered in my ear in the midst of one of our eccentric dances at the Catholic House, Look, all eyes are upon us, so I tried the step Fuksa-Koštálová is known for, but eccentric force landed us under a table, Jarmilka once tried to do at the Slávia what she'd seen at the Ziegfeld Follies, but she misjudged the lunge and sailed over my head and rammed her glasses so deep into an eyebrow you can still see the scar, Vlasta of the Havrda girls was my favorite though, she was madly in love with me, once when I was carrying her around a nightclub on my shoulders she laughed so hard she wet both herself and me and the whole place went into an uproar, people say she died in a car accident with a bunch of soldiers, but Havrda says it's not true, she's still alive, too much alive, and working as a nurse, in any case she was so temperamental she belonged in a convent, I'd bought a nose straightener at the time, you wore it on your nose the way women wear curlers in their hair, you screwed it on according to the kind of nose you had in mind, I wanted one like Rudolph Valentino's, Havrda used to play cards with an old man named Švec, God's Blessings was their game, and as Švec was walking past a church near the end of his life he said to himself, I wonder what they do in there, he'd never set foot in a church before, and seeing all the pomp he said, A pity no one ever told me, and decided to stay on as a sacristan, that was about the time when Vlasta threw the handsome miller's ring back in his face, I never bought her anything, I just took her a rose now and then, that disarms a woman, the minute I entered the pub she'd come and sit next to me, I'd make believe I was reading the paper and she'd say, What are you doing sitting there like a toadstool? and I'd press her against a pillar and the waiter would run to her rescue and I'd kick him away like a football and lean over her like a hero and give her a kiss, and the pub would go wild, some pharmacies sold Fountain of Youth steambath facials, another gold-medal

winner and as elegant as they come, with the head
of a pretty woman on the box-top, she was under
a kind of brooding basket connected by a nickel
tube to a bronze machine and had on a Brussels
lace blouse with EVER YOUNG crocheted across the
breast, one night one of my beauties came up to
me behind the record player on Žofín Island and
whispered, What do you say we get out of here,
the two of us, I'll just give my face a scrub and
put on some fresh underwear, you wouldn't believe how jealous those vamps were, they even
tried to poison my coffee, it was about the time
me and old man Řepa were delivering beer with
a team of oxen, and one day the oxen lay down
on the tracks and the gatekeeper couldn't lower
the barrier, so the train just stood there and the
engine drivers jumped down and the conductors
tried pulling the beasts by their tails, but they just
lay there, and soon the train was ten minutes behind schedule and all the conductor could do was
count each extra minute on his pocket watch, the

stationmaster's assistant waved a rug-beater in front of them, but they kept chewing their cud, then a milkman remembered the thing to do was squirt water in their ears, and that did it, up came their tails and off they bolted at such a pace that we lost a few kegs in the curves and the boss threw a fit and said, Here, take my bike and get me a pack of Egypts, so I took the bike and pushed it all the way to the shop and back, and when I gave him the cigarettes he yelled, Where have you been so long? and I said, I don't know how to ride a bike, and who should show up just then but Zdenka, all decked out like the pope and desirous of a private audience with me, so off we went to the workers' dormitory, all the men from the brewery thought I'd knocked her up and I just wanted her to see the picture over my bunk showing a man by the name of Othello murdering his beloved, but Zdenka stretched a blanket across the window, so the boss ordered two men to lean a ladder against the wall and he climbed up, I could see his face over the blanket and a rain cloud, black as pitch in the middle, with a golden border, and sitting there on my bunk I told Zdenka the story of how Kaluža and Kalíř arrested Lecián and how when Lecián was up there on the gallows he said to Wohlschleger, his hangman, Get on with it, your hands are cold, and Zdenka said, Married life with you would be bliss, but I talked her out of it, I told her I lacked the criminal instincts for matrimony, because when children start coming you're really in for it, then even the emperor jumps out of bed at night, which is why Schumann the composer waded into cold water and said to his wife in the movie, People are puppets, that's where inspiration comes from, but when your piece is ready you can go for a schnapps or a stroll, and when Zdenka tried to get me on my back by saying a hundred crowns would do the trick, I told her Mr. Batista's book said a virgin is always best and kissing distance is bliss and not even us soldiers

were in the habit of climbing through windows
and raping innocent girls, at least that's what
Colonel Zawada taught us, and he had eight
horses and thirty-six infantry battalions shot out
from under him, when I told that to a young
woman she giggled and said it was no wonder
we'd lost on all fronts, we were a degenerate
army, Colonel Zawada had a German shepherd
and two batteries of cannons, the enemy was all
over the woods, trees were going up like matches,
but Colonel Zawada studied his maps and put
machine guns in all the hot places, he wore a gold
collar with a big star on it and kept having us
practice enemy attacks, he would take me by the
chin and make sure I was well shaven and only
then inspect my weapons, at three in the morning
we'd get coffee and at five we'd go and relieve the
front line, first the bugler, next the drummer, and
lastly the officers flying all over the place, by then
it had stopped raining, Zdenka sat there drawing
pictures on the floor with her umbrella and the

boss stood there shading his eyes and peeking in
on us, but Zdenka told me to come and see her
that evening, she wanted to show me her striped
featherbed and play me her new records, The Silver Fern and a characteristic intermezzo called
The Black Forest Mill, and as she walked down
the path the brewers drooled like Saint Bernards
to see so firm and fully packed a toy of nature
and the boss stared after her through his telescope
and I swung a shovel over my shoulder and went
out to turn the barley, thinking of Smetana, who
was more slave than master and when he died
they used his music for wrapping sausages, two
cases full, that's what you get for helping your
people to enjoy their leisure time, which is what
Dvořák was after too, and he was a butcher's apprentice, but no, all people want to do is drink
and listen to Humoresque, when the police came
for Havlíček his wife Juliánka thought she'd go
out of her mind or her heart would break, the
head that man Havlíček had on him, the epigrams

he wrote, the epistles, Bondy the poet once went
to see my nephew, with his two babies in their
baby buggy and because the pub closed after
they'd drunk only three buckets of beer they took
one home for the night and poured it into the
washbasin and went on with their academic debate till they fell asleep, and my nephew woke up
thinking a pipe had burst, but it was only poor
Bondy pissing his two buckets onto the rug, after
which he tumbled back into bed and didn't get
up until morning when the babies began to bawl,
and he looked around and shouted Eureka! out
of the blue and started cheering and jumping up
and down on the piss-soaked rug and shouting,
Listen, everybody, not only people who aren't
with us are with us, no, even people who are
against us are with us, because you can't cut yourself off from your times, there you have it, ladies,
now you see why poets love to drink and medi-
tate, and just when things are looking grim the
heavens open up and out comes a thought making

its way to the light, I kept turning the raging malt I'd plowed up and thinking, Socrates and Christ they never wrote a line yet their teachings are still valid, while others are less read the more books they publish, history's revenge you might call it, I once challenged a soapmaker to a diving contest from a billiard table and won, though my head was full of bumps and bruises afterwards, one day we reenacted King Farouk's triumphant march, all the bar beauties took part even though it was engineered by that bastard Olánek who sold second-hand furniture and paintings and who once took a painting and made a hole in it just where the Virgin Mary's eye was and put an eye from a carp in the hole and made it stick with a piece of adhesive on the back, and the Hungarians he sold it to hung it next to the stove and one day they ran out and told everybody they'd been praying to the Virgin Mary and she'd started shedding tears over them when all that really happened was the carp's eye had burst, anyway, that

bastard Olának brought a donkey into the Tunnel
Bar and the bar beauties undressed me and pulled
a kind of slip over me, wound a turban round my
head, smeared my face with enamel paint, and
took me from pub to pub on the donkey—the
Grand was the only one we got kicked out of—
and then that bastard Olának gave the donkey
pepper to smell and it threw me, but I was still a
hero, I went to the zoo dressed in a fine suit I'd
inherited from a man whose legs were so crooked
he had to have his trousers made to measure, but
otherwise they fit as if made for a dollar Venus,
so anyway there I was standing in front of the
lion's cage and all at once the lion lets loose and
psss! I get this beer-glass worth of lion piss bril-
liantine in my hair, he managed to hit two Slo-
venes too, I had to use perfume for a week the
stink was so bad, and the City Bar beauties kept
sniffing me and asking if I hadn't been hanging
around their competition, there wasn't any television or even radio at the time so people had to

do everything for themselves, and they lived one on top of the other, poor people never let their beds cool down, they took turns sleeping in them, the man on night shift in a hotel would climb into a warm bed when the man on day shift went off to work, once a group of rabbit breeders invited me to demonstrate my vocal art and I decided to perform The Nightingale Trills on the Shore for their enjoyment, but that bastard Olánek told the band to play something else, so it was me and my Nightingale against them and their Joyful Youth, well, the rabbit breeders were hopping mad and threw the bowl with the lottery tickets at me and a Wiener schnitzel too, but I was still a hero, I was sorting potatoes one day for my brother, the one I went to visit for two weeks, and his boss saw me and said, What's this maltster doing lying fallow? and he shoved a shovel into my hands and soon I was demonstrating the high-quality techniques I'd learned at the Benešov brewery of Oliverius & Šarlinger, which really floored him, so then he asked me how I was at unloading coal, and I grabbed another shovel and before you could blink an eye the coal was rolling at his feet and by the time he shouted, Hey, man, watch what you're doing, he was up to his knees in it, but I just kept going and in only three quarters of an hour I was through, You don't waste any time, do you? his beauty of a bookkeeper said to me, and I said, You mean this? this is child's play, I got my training from Římský, the strongman of Kokory, who kicked a young lady's wooden leg to bits during a brawl, after which four policemen died in their hospital beds, it's a real talent going straight for the jugular or smashing an Adam's apple or placing the wrench between the eyes, and my brother's boss said, Your reward will be to go beeing with me, and he put on his bee veil and gloves, because a swarm of bees is no laughing matter, the bees make these big bumps on a tree and they have to be cut off, which the tree owners don't like, so you get into fights with your neighbors,

anyway, my brother's boss told me he wanted to
teach me and Mr. Haňka how to hang out bee-
hives, but while we were having our first lesson
Mr. Haňka tripped and dropped one and off we
flew, but little good it did us, they lit into us
something awful, Mr. Haňka knelt and begged
the bees to stop, he had a wife and children, but
they stung him all over, even his private parts,
which swelled up to the size of a watering can, I
couldn't go to the bar for three days, and the first
thing Bobinka did when she saw me was to play
Cemetery, Cemetery on the Victrola, and the next
thing was to take me upstairs—because she didn't
think I could see much yet—and strip me naked,
then she filled a pitcher with water and said, How
about a little marriage training using the Hardy
method, but all at once we heard a scream outside
the door, well, what had happened was the blacksmith was so drunk they foisted a real hag off on
him, but he switched on his flashlight and burst
out of the room in his underpants, smashing the

railing to smithereens and shouting, Who gave me that old bat? she's as ugly as an academic portrait painter! well, I threw on my clothes then and there, I was as sensitive as the blacksmith, it wasn't at all like the time when we initiated the stove fitter into the mysteries of love on the billiard table, he was a little crack-brained to begin with, he'd tiled himself twice into stoves and had to be pried out with a crowbar, which meant redoing the entire stove, even now the daughters of good families bring me roses and wonder how I came by my good manners, but you should have seen what Olánek did when we wished him a happy fiftieth birthday and asked him how his health was holding up, right there in the main square he pulled out his member—he had ten beers in him at the time—and drenched the advertisement for Náchod Mills all the way to the accent over the *a* while the local notary public passed under the stream and wished us a pleasant day, then there was the long-distance pissing

contest at the Terrace Bar, Olánek was sure he'd
won when a man who looked like nothing if not
a Mariazell beggar piped up and asked if he could
have a go at it, and Olánek said all right provided
the winner got a liter of French cognac, so that
night at midnight there were two bottles of cognac on the table, and the two men stepped out
onto the terrace and the other guy undid his fly
and in a flash the house across the road was drip-
ping wet, you could hear the piss sloshing into
the Elbe, so Olánek backed off and the other guy
took his two bottles and disappeared, and Vít,
who played drums in the navy band, said to No-
vák the violinist, How about a round of Violetta,
and everybody climbed up on their chairs and I
performed The Sultan's Wedding and Olánek
tried to patch up his reputation by doing tableaux
vivants on the table and pissing out over the
guests, a lady told me later it would serve me
right if I got hauled into court for mixing with
the likes of him, one day I went to hear Járinek

Pospíšil sing at the National Hall and the first
thing he did was to ask whether there were any
singers in the house, well, the ladies they all
shouted, You go! to me, so the famous tenor
helped me up onto the stage and told me to take
a seat, but I said I couldn't, and suddenly the audience was all abuzz, so he said, Why not? and I
said, Because I only paid for standing room, well,
you should have heard the women shriek, I had
one-upped the great Pospíšil! and then the piano
chimed in and I sang The Painful Farewell and
the ladies nearly brought the house down, what
they said about Pospíšil was that even though he
was divorced he had a voice like a nightingale and
people like him shouldn't serve in the army because it would be a great loss to the nation if they
were killed in a war, which I understood very
well, because in the days of the monarchy I carried Captain Tonser's saber, I even had the good
fortune to see the Generals von Manteuffel and
von Rosenegg sitting together in a car wearing

their gold helmets that looked liked chamber pots
topped with the spikes they used to use for spruc-
ing up china cupboards, I was also present when
the two marshals with their pince-nez, Auffen-
berg and Dankl, launched the first offensive, and
I had the honor of holding Conrad von Hötzendorf's bridle or, rather, his horse's bridle, an
old man he was, but straight as a young lady, his
son died in the marshes at the Battle of Goro-
denka, if they'd only stayed put, what were they
doing gallivanting around anyway? Conrad von
Hötzendorf was a member of the emperor's family, an archduke, so he wore a little sheep around
his neck like the emperor, only the emperor's
held its head up and Conrad von Hötzendorf's
held its head down, I've had quite a few dreams
about monkeys, which according to Anna Nováková means you're going to be either seriously
ill or lucky in love, but I've also dreamed of a
dagger plunged into a chest, which means love
requited, one day during Mass our priest turned

and looked for the sexton, where was he? why
wasn't he serving? why was he ruining the Mass?
well, the sexton had slipped off to the pub for a
quick nip instead of pouring the three teaspoons
of incense into the censer so the priest could wave
it through the church, incense is a resin that
comes all the way from Africa, myrrh and aloe,
anyway, the sexton comes back a little tipsy from
his crème de menthe and the priest, taking the
chalice out of the tabernacle, asks him, Where
have you been? and the sexton says, I had to go
to the toilet, and the priest puts down the chalice
and bam! gives him a swift kick and shouts,
Hasn't anybody ever told you that during the di-
vine liturgy you are my right-hand man and that
you don't pop out for a crème de menthe? and
after a few more kicks and some punches in the
nose for good measure he picks up the chalice and
goes on with the service, and the women all sat
there wondering about the new ritual they'd wit-
nessed, and you know what, ladies? the sexton

stopped going to the church after that and turned into a model social democrat, people used to be awfully nervous, if you dreamed someone was pouring cucumbers over your head from a plate it meant ardent love, or if you dreamed of a hag it meant marriage would stay away from your door, my brother was apprenticed to a baker from Valašsko, a man by the name of Benda, and once when he didn't catch something this Benda had said he said, What? and the next thing he knew he was flat on the ground, and when he came to this Benda said to him he said, Where I come from we say, I beg your pardon, but eventually he went to the dogs, he inherited some money from his mother and started drinking and ended up freezing to death somewhere, not a pretty story, it was like giving a child a knife to play with, our priest had the misfortune of finding a boy going at it with a girl one night right next to the church, at first he was afraid it was a parish priest, but it wasn't, anyway, he reported

it, and soon we had a visit from four football
players, at least that's what the missionaries sent
to inspect local morals looked like in their cas-
socks and string belts, and they improved the local morals to such an extent that the police had
to be called in, because the social democrats asked
them very disturbing questions about man coming from the ape, and the freethinkers started
arguing with them over which came first, the
chicken or the egg, and on they went for two
hours—where does the chicken come from? the
egg, and where does the egg come from? the
chicken—until somebody shouted, And where
does the first egg come from? and the freethinkers
yelled, From nature! and the missionaries yelled,
Which God created! and before long they were
knocking each other's blocks off and the church
ladies ran and got the cops and said those godless
atheists were insulting the sons of God, and then
the ladies started throwing stones at the freethinkers but hit two cops, because you can't close

God up in a box, can you? now I remember, if you dream of plowing it means a wedding is in the offing, if you dream of striking matches it means you're in love, Mr. Batista's book says a twenty-year-old beauty gives any healthy young man a charge though she's no more use to an old man than an overcoat is to a corpse, our major was sitting on his stallion one day, surveying the most beautiful army in the world, and what does he see but a soldier in an overcoat covered with blood, so he calls him out of formation and bawls out the man's sergeant for having such filthy troops, in the days of the monarchy barons put up mirrors in their horses' stalls but let their grooms and servant girls sleep in the lofts, day laborers lived worse than cattle, yet somehow people sang more, maybe to make the work go faster, people don't sing anymore when they work, my friend Římský had a quick temper and a quick fist, when he went into a pub people's hearts sank into their boots, one day Římský fidgeted a little after the command Habt acht! and the lieutenant ran over to him and gave him a punch in the stomach, well, that was his chance, he grabbed the lieutenant's sword and broke it over his knee, then gave him an uppercut to the jaw and laid him out flat, the officers made a run for it, but the men were tickled pink, Prince Liechtenstein had a hundred estates, but to keep from paying taxes and raising his own army he merged them into ninety-nine, on the other hand, the doctors had to amputate his member and insert a silver tube in its place, so you see, young ladies, you can have all the riches in the world and still lack what matters most, which is why you need to take Mr. Batista's words into account and never buy a pig in a poke, you never know how things will turn out, one man takes up with a tramp and gets off scot-free, another takes all the proper precautions and gets a disease, one woman jumps off a ladder but still can't get rid of her baby, another blows her nose too hard and

loses it, then there's the courting game, a clever
girl puts an ad in the paper, seeking a man of
sterling character, and, say, I respond, but just to
make certain she checks up on me, asks around,
he's not a skirtchaser, is he? she even goes to
a detective agency for more information, really
now! when I was in the army some dummy filled
a bottle with pitralon thinking it was hypermangan, and one of the men coming back from the
ladies washed himself off with what he thought
was hypermangan but what was actually pitralon,
well, you should have seen him race through the
barracks lowing like a cow that needed milking,
the same thing happened to our grandmother
with a tonic the doctor had made up for her, a
brown liquid she kept in a bottle next to the mirror, but our Great Dane was having trouble with
its leg at the time and it had a brown salve in a
bottle next to the mirror, well, one day Grandma
drank the dog's salve with a blissful smile on her
face because her tonic was part raspberry juice,

and the minute she swallowed it we had to run
for the doctor and then for the priest, a beauty
once asked me very discreetly to take her urine
to the doctor, but the doctor jumped down my
throat and said she had to bring it on her own,
though people tend to like me, Don't go yet, they
tell me, we don't yet know why you're here, I
was especially popular at church fairs, Make sure
you come now, they'd say, We need somebody
to clobber, they were just joking of course, I remember standing on a bridge holding hands with
a beauty, looking down at the waves and up at
the brown sky, and telling her that our town has
thirty-two pubs, twenty-eight of which come
with ladies, and is theater-crazy enough to have
five theaters, the best plays were done at the
Catholic Hall by a traveling company called the
Přemysl Players, their biggest hit was El Tigro, a
Mexican operetta starring a farmhand by the
name of Kopecký who so strained himself har-
vesting clover that they had to stretch him out on

a ladder and walk up and down him before each
performance, then everything was fine except he
had trouble standing after going down on his
knees to declare his love, still he never failed to
sing the role with great passion, and once he sang
with such passion that his fly split open, which
caused a real sensation, the ladies talked of nothing else all week, a group of tinkers and lock-
smiths put on plays at the National Hall, plays
about aristocrats mostly, Lady Wantoch's Fan or
Lady Winter's Fan or something like that, anyway the lord was played by a sign painter, and
when he knelt the striped trousers that went with
the frock coat slid up and you could see his long
johns underneath, and when he came out for his
bows he was hit in the head by the lead weight
that brought the curtain up and down, the ladies
went wild when they saw him lying there, they
thought it was part of the play, and at a performance of The Pearls of the Maiden Serafina in
Hálek the director peeked through a hole in the

curtain to see if people had taken their seats and then signaled to the stage manager to raise the curtain, but because the stage manager had been weaned on the foamy brew he raised the director together with the curtain, and when the director fell into the orchestra pit the audience applauded what they thought was the opening scene, and when they put on Raduz and Mahulena, which begins in the dark, the stage manager pulled up the curtain too soon and Raduz didn't realize it was up and asked, Where are you, Mahulena? and she called out from her branch, Up shit creek, and the audience was tickled pink again, they figured they were in for something racy from life, but when the stage manager saw what he'd done he gave the cord a jerk and the curtain came whizzing down and practically chopped Raduz's head off and the stage manager switched the house lights on and stuck his head through the curtain and shouted, The cord snapped! oh that was a fine show that was! but the best show of all was the

Catholic Hall production of A Midsummer Night's Dream with the Přemysl Players, who all had their heads shaved for the occasion and one of the fairies got sciatica because it was winter, they counted all their jumps and used flashlights for lighting, but the character who wears the ass's head fell into the orchestra pit and started shouting Die, die! and the audience burst into applause, a standard bearer in our regiment, a man as strong as the Bauer who lifted cows over his head for fun and beat Frištenský, asked me to be his enemy on the parade ground one day when we were practicing Parade rechts and Parade links and single combat with fixed bayonets, so we got into position and I lunged then and there and pow! whacked him on the chin with my bayonet, which had this little ball on the end of it, and he did a backward somersault and had to be given artificial respiration by the Bosnians, You could have killed him, the lieutenants yelled at me, but I said, He asked me to be his enemy, but the lieutenants said, You should have done Parade rechts and Parade links first and only then gone into the einfacher Stoss, but I said, Really now, you don't expect me to do Parade rechts and Parade links with my enemy! of course I went straight to the einfacher Stoss, that was what made me a hero, there was a woman in our town by the name of Kača Rypová, a giant she was and a terrific dancer and when it came to beer she could drink anybody under the table, but one day this joker spiked her beer with mercury and then asked her to dance, it was a horrible sight, let me tell you, her daughter was a strange one though, her and her husband they'd go at it on the floor with their kids watching, I saw them too because I once made a delivery there and looked in through the window, but what I liked more than anything was the Mohammedan heaven with beauties on every floor, Mohammedans have something to look forward to, while Catholics must wonder what it's all for, when they get to their heaven all they

seem to do is stare at the sun, Jesus! said Bondy
the poet when one of his kids fell out of the baby
buggy as we were leaving the pub, Jesus H.
Christ! why is it some people buy prime pork for
a song and I pay five hundred for a slice of bread?
the slow train out of Steinbruck wasn't running
one day so they put me on the fast train and it
had this conductor who immediately caught my
eye, a real looker, the Sýkorová type, well, before
I knew it I was in first class, anyone else she
would have thrown out or given a whack on the
nose with her ticket punch but me she offered an
Egypt, and when this unshaven worker type with
a pipe hanging out of his mouth came into the
compartment, she said, Beat it, buster, you're in
third class, and chased him out, but I said, I'm in
third class too, and she rubbed her knee against
mine and whispered in my ear, What do you say
we paint the town pink you and me when we get
to Vienna, women can be so forward and Polish
women take the cake, one of them just wouldn't

get off my hospital bed, the doctor called her a
slut and a whore, her name was Jadwiga and she
liked men better than food, when I told my stories at the pub the police would take off their
holsters and belts, You've got the charm of a marriage swindler, they told me, and I'd grab one of
their bayonets and sharpen the waitress's pencil
with it just like Chaplin, and I wouldn't go back
to the brewery till I'd made the rounds of the
pubs, nobody ever said a word because I'd have
sailed back over the wall and made the rounds
again, once a group of businessmen came and ordered wine and liqueurs and a soldier climbed up
on the billiard table and did tableaux vivants in-
cluding dangling a bucket of water from his member, a genuine virtuoso in other words, the ladies
remember it to this day, one of the businessmen
bought me a cigar that made me sick and I col-
lapsed and the policemen carted me back to the
brewery like a roll of linoleum, Konůpek, the engine driver who played the helicon—a helicon's

an instrument with a mouthpiece like a chamber pot—anyway, Konůpek used to say that serious music takes a lot of muscle and he had a neck like a bull, one day his grandfather was coming out of the woods on his way home from a church fair where he'd been playing the helicon when a gust of wind twisted the helicon on its strap and he choked to death, and one day Dubovský the goldsmith started wondering what his daughter was doing with her fiancé when he was out, so he told her he was going to the pictures but crawled under the couch instead and heard her come in with him and saw his boots and felt the springs come down on his stomach as they sat on the couch, and then he saw some clothes fall and some underclothes and the boots swing up, but more Dubovský the goldsmith did not see, because one of the couch springs rammed into his neck, and shout as he might they heard not a word because they were shouting too, and not until much later did they roll away the couch and